More

Radio Shows That

Are Fiction

Joseph De Lucia

MORE RADIO SHOWS THAT ARE FICTION BY JOSEPH DE LUCIA

ISBN 978-0-615-16768-8

# More Radio Shows That Are Fiction

ISBN 978-0-615-16768-8

Pastor Enoch: No. I realized I was a sinner at two and a half years old, and I have walked with God ever since the day I repented. Preaching always came easy for me. I practiced on the anyone who would listen to me. They laughed until I got my Doctorate Degree in Ministry.

Announcer: Tell the listening audience about yourself.

Pastor Enoch: I was known as a baby preacher, since I was so young. It seems I've always walked with God, and am never weary of the adventure.

Announcer: You've always been about the Lord's work. What do you do for diversity?

Pastor Enoch: When I don't preach I travel to different parts of the world giving speeches on college campuses. And I make time to paint at least one scene from every city I've ever been in.

2
5

Announcer:  You must have an impressive collection!

Pastor Enoch: I painted Paris, France and other cities in countries I can't remember. I did visit the most popular places, though. I assembled the paintings in an artbook called Enoch's Travels: The Paintings. The book of one-hundred of my best paintings sell for $79.95 at fine art stores all over the world.

Announcer:  What else have you been doing?

Pastor Enoch: I am taking acting lessons so I can belier portray the characters in the Bible. I noticed the people in the local church pay more attention when I put on a wig and a robe and some make-up.

Announcer:  Is it difficult being a preacher in the late nineties?

Pastor Enoch: Not at all. If I'm criticized, I just tune it all out and go on with my ministry. The critics are all thorns in my

Announcer: You must have an impressive collection!

Pastor Enoch: I painted Paris, France and other cities in countries I can't remember. I did visit the most popular places, though. I assembled the paintings in an artbook called Enoch's Travels: The Paintings. The book of one-hundred of my best paintings sell for $79.95 at fine art stores all over the world.

Announcer: What else have you been doing?

Pastor Enoch: I am taking acting lessons so I can beffer portray the characters in the Bible. I noticed the people in the local church pay more affention when I put on a wig and a robe and some make-up.

Announcer: Is it difficult being a preacher in the late nineties?

Pastor Enoch: Not at all. If I'm criticized, I just tune it all out and go on with my ministry. The critics are all thorns in my flesh, and I don't live by their evaluation of my work.

I decided to close my ears to all hurtful words that attempt to tear me down. I'm on earth to encourage everyone. Too bad if some people would rather not listen.

Announcer: I listened to one of your sermons on cassette last night. You read a poem called <u>I Shall Someday Be With Him</u>. Will you read a few lines for our listening audience?

Pastor Enoch: I'd love to. I shall someday be with Him, to see Him, face to face. I shall one day be in Heaven- I have run life's difficult race, with Him.

Announcer: Tell the radio audience what the poem means to you.

Pastor Enoch: Seeing our Lord, face to face, has always been my goal. Since Heaven is God's Home I asked Jesus to live in me, so I

can walk through The Pearly Gates. I am still in the difficult race of life. It is easier since He is always encouraging me. I look forward to eternity with Him.

Announcer: I understand you play the saxaphone, and that you have a CD called Pastor Enoch's Sweet Saxaphone.

Pastor Enoch: Yes, I use all my talents to glorify the Lord. The CD has been mass produced and is sold for $19.95 in bookstores and music stores all over the world.

Announcer: Everyone should use the talents he has to glorify the Lord.

Pastor Enoch: How true. How true.

Announcer: Did you ever lose interest in spiritual things?

2
8

Pastor Enoch: I did have one low point in my life where I needed to get away from everyone and everything. I flew my plane to the most remote island I could find, for seven months. All I did was watch the sun rise in the morning, and set in the evening. In between sunrise and sunset all I did was walk and walk. I walk the island every day and night--hot or cold, sunshine or rain. When I came back home from my leave of absence I felt very refreshed. I felt like a new person. I was told the quality of my sermons improved quite a lot.

Announcer: Do you recommend a leave of absence for everyone?

Pastor Enoch: No, it isn't for everyone. It is only for the workaholics like me who don't know when to stop. As much as I like my job, I needed the outdoors. I needed to be alone, and not worry about praying for anyone's needs. I needed to not be taken for granted. I'm not this Sunday pulpit

fixture spouting sermons. I left only to return with the revival spirit in my bones.

Announcer: You're listening to WCHR, 77.7 on your A.M. radio dial.

RADIO SHOW FOR JUNE 16th, 1997

Announcer: Pastor Felix, welcome to our humble studio! People, this is Pastor Felix, from Paris, France. He came to share a few words of how God's working in his life.

Pastor Felix: As you may have read in your local newspaper I encourage everyone to read the Bible. I also challenge everyone to check out the Bible prophecies, and the cities that are mentioned in the Bible. I also teach people how to read, and write, for free.

Announcer: You have a four-fold ministry. It seems God is blessing you in the church

Announcer: What does the poem mean to you?

Pastor Felix: We should all read the Bible until it becomes a part of us, and we can faithfully live the verses that apply to our walk with our Lord.

Announcer: What if people insist that the Bible is all fables and fictional stories?

Pastor Felix: I just pray for them that God will deal with their hearts. I got a letter a few weeks ago by an atheist that was dying of lung cancer. R. R. of Cleveland, Oregon writes: :"Pastor Felix, I regret not listening to the wisdom of your columns. I never read the Bible and refused to until you wrote a column that began, 'I am praying all the time for people to take off their sunglasses and see the light.' I took my sunglasses off and am seeing the light. I decided to renounce my unbelief and am living my last days to serve the Lord! Thank you.

3
2

Announcer: What a testimony to how God worked in your life, so you could touch another lifeI

Pastor Felix: Even though our sermons are not always palatable, we, as men of God, never use the pulpit for our own personal forum to express views that are unbiblical. The pulpit is a holy place meant only for the Word of God.

Announcer: You sing like Pavarotti, don't you?

Pastor Felix: I sing my heart out to the Lord. I tried to sing alto, but it always came out tenor.

Announcer: I read in Music Today that you wrote a gospel opera called Surrendered To Our Lord. What is it about?

Pastor Felix: A hard hearted man hears a moving sermon at a Billy Graham Crusade

3
3

and gives his heart to the Lord. The opera is a follow up on his life as he gets older. The man is converted at twenty and his life is in operatic form every five years till he~ s sixty. I loved writing it.

Announcer: Good for you. And God bless.

Pastor Felix: I wrote a book of short stories, too.
Can I tell you about them?

Announcer: Be my guest.

Pastor Felix: I wrote some short stories about the fruit of the Spirit in the lives of Christians of different ages and different incomes, in different parts of the world.

Announcer: Is the book fiction, or non☐fiction? And what is the book called?

Pastor Felix: It is a non-fiction book entitled Sharing The Fruit. Spiritual men, woman,

3
4

Pastor Gabriel: How original.

Announcer: I understand you moon-light as a part-time car mechanic. Right?

Pastor Gabriel: Yes, it is. I love the sound of smooth running engines. And when they don't run smooth, I make sure to trouble□shoot every problem 'till the cars run like new.

Announcer: And you pastor a church full time? What's the name of your church?

Pastor Gabriel: The Church Of Continuous Healing.

Announcer: Do you always have healing services?

Pastor Gabriel: We never have any healing services at the church. People just get healed---no invitations, no laying on of

hands, no prayers for the sick. When God says to a person "Be well" the formerly sick person gets out of the chair and gives a testimony.

Announcer:  How does it happen?

Pastor Gabriel: No one knows. Probably because the church has such a sweet spirit to it. Sometimes on Sunday mornings we just sit and wait for the Lord to move. Once He moves in our hearts the sermon flows like living water and the hardened hearts are softened by the constant love of every person in the church.

Announcer:  Love is powerful, isn't it?

Pastor Gabriel: But God's love through us is power multiplied many, many times.

Announcer:  Amen!

Pastor Gabriel: I came across this poem in an anthology when I needed to put the

Word in a more concrete light. It is called
He Has Given So
Much To Me. Can I read a few lines for your
listeners?

Announcer: I'd love to hear you read a few
lines.

Pastor Gabriel: He has given so much to me,
what have I given to Him, in return; He has
given me His love, What love have I shown to
Him, in return.

Announcer: What does that poem mean to
you? How did it touch your heart?

Pastor Gabriel: The poet talks about the
abundance of things received of the Lord,
especially His love. It is very difficult for any
one to give the Lord a gift, unless it is our
lives so He could use. The poet also asks
rhetorically if he has shown the Lord any love
at all.

3
8

The poem touched my heart by helping me to face the fact that I don't love the Lord as much as I should. I need to be thank Him more often for the little blessings in life, the blessings that we take for granted.

Announcer: That was well said. Thank you. And you are tuned to <u>WCHR</u>, 77.7 on your A.M. radio dial. Pastor, what would you like to leave our audience with?

Pastor Gabriel: Folks, just remember to give your all to the Lord, and, if you can't ask Him to help you.

Announcer: Could you share a few personal stories from your ministry?

Pastor Gabriel: Sure. One time as I was preaching a sermon called Asking God For Directions In Life, a member of the congregation called out from the pews, "I need specific guidance in how to live my life!" All I said was, "Read the Bible, and

pray." The member said, "I will." He ended up being a Bible scholar at the
local seminary, since he saw himself as called to the ministry, loving people to the Lord.

Announcer: This is WCHR, 77.7 on your A.M. radio dial.

RADIO SHOW FOR JUNE 18th, 1997

Announcer: We have In our studios today Pastor Hosea, from a liftle church in Hawaii called The Completely Delivered Church Of Celebration. How goes it in Hawaii, Pastor?

Pastor Hosea: Wonderful! God is blessing us by leaps and bounds. We don't promise a thing at the church, the Lord just delivers people in the twinkling of an eye.

Announcer: No altar call? No singing? Nothing?

Pastor Hosea: I just expect the Lord to deliver who-ever He wants to, and He does.

Announcer: Don't you pray?

Pastor Hosea: All we ever do is drench the church in prayer. Maybe that's why God is moving in Hawaii.

Announcer: And all over the world.

Pastor Hosea: So true! So true!

Announcer: Do you have any hobbies?

Pastor Hosea: I design houses for the fun of it.

Announcer: Did you go to school to learn this?

Pastor Hosea: No, I just asked the Lord to help me to design houses of worship for Him, and I've been doing it for five years already.

Announcer: You must have a vivid imagination!

Pastor Hosea: That I do. The designs come to me in a flash. Once I start drawing I can't stop. The best church I designed was one called The Heavenly Saint Church Of Saved Souls. I did compile all my designs in a book called Hosea's

Houses Of Worship. It sells for $125.00 at fine art stores everywhere. I make sure the important things like windows and roofs are all top quality. I suggest that old lighting and old carpet are used. I've saved the churches hundreds by even insisting that old chairs made of steel is better than expensive pews. We are here to worship God, and not lust after pretty church decor.

Announcer: You're saying that the church should look decent, but not cost the people a ton of money, right?

Pastor Hosea: Exactly! If the church wastes God's money, then it encourages the people to waste God's money. As a result, tithing will go way down and the local church will suffer.

Announcer: But, this view is yours. It does not reflect the view of 77.7, WCHR and Its staff or management.

Pastor Hosea: It is my opinion, for what its worth.

Announcer: I understand you're quite a golfer!

Pastor Hosea: I need to do something when I'm not in the pulpit. Besides, I always give the glory to God when I come close to a hole in one.

Announcer: And when you have a bad day on the course?

Pastor Hosea: I just grin and bear it, knowing it can't get any worse.

Announcer: Good affitude!

Pastor Hosea: It isn't easy. I did get so mad one time I said 'DARN' real loud. I guess I blew my cool, calm testimony that day.

Announcer: I said darn once and my wife sewed every hole in every one of my ripped shirts and torn pants.

Pastor Hosea: Whatever you say. Can I share I song I wrote called I Want My Loved Ones To Be Saved.

Announcer: What a sweet title for a song! Please, sing for our listening audience.

4
4

Pastor Hosea: I want my loved ones to be saved,

      to know the Lord as their Savior, to pray to Him always, to worship Him with their lives.

Announcer: Nice song! I'm sure it will be sung by many recording artists all over the world.

Pastor Hosea: I put my all into this song, just like with my preaching. I came across a poem called Holy Spirit Conviction. Can I read part of it?

Announcer: It's an interesting title for a poem. You can read it any time you're ready.

Pastor Hosea: Upon sermons preached from the Word of God, the Holy Spirit convicts men who will repent of their sins; Upon reading the Bible, men can come to know the Lord as Savior, Will they respond to God's

Spirit. Upon songs sung at a tent revival, the Holy Spirit

4
5

will convict men who will respond to the Lord's voice.

Announcer: What does this poem mean to you?

Pastor Hosea: It isn't possible for a man to get saved without the Holy Spirit's help.

Announcer: What else would you like to share with the listening audience?

Pastor Hosea: Don't give up praying for your friends and relatives to get saved. It takes constant prayer to show the Lord that you care about the eternity of your most loved ones.

Announcer: Fasting helps, too.

Pastor Hosea: Prayer and fasting is a good combination. But, nothing should be over done. All things in moderation.

4
6

Announcer: And you're listening to <u>WCHR</u>, 77.7 on your A.M. radio dial. We are also on the Internet, the letters are www. wchr. comm. Write us soon to let us know you are listening.

RADIO SHOW FOR JUNE 19th, 1997

Announcer: We have in our studio today Pastor lmrah from Chicago, Illinois. Welcome, Pastor I.

Pastor lmrah: Thank you. I pastor a church in Chicago called The Winning Souls For Jesus Revival Church.

Announcer: That says it all. Your church sounds like its evangelical.

Pastor Imrah: We knock on every one's door, no matter where they live. If they're not home, or if they don't answer, we leave a tract inviting them to our church.

Announcer: I read in an article that you don't have an invitation for salvation or re☐committmenf. All you do is read the Bible for twenty minutes and you let God do all the work.

Pastor lmrah: I never went to Bible School, or Seminary. I just knew how to read the Bible out loud without comment or improper inflections. I've been able to pick up any language in an instant, and read any language flawlessly.

Announcer: What a gift! I'm sure you've been a blessing to other people.

Pastor Imrah: I guess. I just give my talent to the Lord and watch how He uses it.

Announcer: Tell the listening audience about yourself.

Pastor Imrah: Ever since I could talk I began swearing, not knowing what I was

saying. My parents kept telling me to be quiet, but I never could control my tongue. It got so bad that the elders and the deacons of The Pure In Heart Church Of God's Love laid hands on me, and prayed for two hours for me. After their prayers I felt cleansed inside and asked to read a Bible. I've been healed ever since.

Announcer: Wonderful! God works His wonders every day.

Pastor Imrah: I did write a book about my experiences called A Lifetime Of Swearing. It's on sale everywhere for only $29.95.

Announcer: What about vows?

Pastor Imrah: I'd rather not even vow one sentence to the Lord, other than the sacred marriage vows.

Announcer: It seems God takes people seriously when they promise Him anything.

Pastor lmrah: I know. That's why I'd rather be safe, than sorry.

Announcer: Have you wriffen any other books?

Pstor lmrah: I did write another book called The Joy Of Reading The Bible. I tell of all my experiences of my public Bible readings. For example, I've been invited to parks, weddings, funerals, revivals, just so I can read His Word.

Announcer: Do you have anything else you would like to share?

Pastor lmrah: A new Christian sent me a poem to read in the church. It is called Turn To God.
I would like to read a few lines, if I may.

Announcer: You may.

Pastor Imrah: Turn to God, He is always there. Turn to the One who understands your needs; Turn to God, He loves you; Turn to the One you may not know.

Announcer: What does this poem mean to you?

Pastor Imrah: The author expressed his heart believing that God is always there, and that He loves and understands everyone. The author even tells people to turn to the Lord whether they know Him or not.

Announcer: Why do you think the author sent this poem to you?

Pastor lmrah: I think he wanted me to use it in a sermon. It seems that I have to have it pre-approved by the deacons before I share anything other than The Holy Scriptures. Besides, if I were to share the poem, the congregation would forget it anyway. I'd be

asked why I didn't spend the time reading The
Bible.

Announcer: Did the poem bless you?

Pastor lmrah: Yes, it did.

Announcer: Then that's all that matters. As long as you got blessed then you don't need to read it out loud, for the church you lead.

Pastor Imrah: I did write a play once.

Announcer: Tell the listening audience about your play.

Pastor lmrah: I call my play The Three Pastors. One is first is very rich, the second is very poor, and the third is middle-class. It takes place at a preacher's convention where all three are thrown together into a small group that compares notes on their particular ministries.

Announcer: Has it been produced by anyone?

Pastor Imrah: It's on Public Access. The play has received a lot of criticism and little praise. I don't understand how people could see a fictional play as a documentary. More people should think about what they say before they say it. Besides, it was meant to be a comedy, but it came out as a drama. There was such a demand for it though, that it's sold on CD, on cassette, and on video. We are also puffing together an interactive CD where the imaginary preachers have interchangeable characters, where each switches into the other's roll. The interactive CD might be less dramatic, and getting my point across.

Announcer: What's the purpose of your play?

Pastor Imrah: The purpose is to show that God loves people no matter how much money is in their pocket.

Announcer: You are listening to <u>WCHR</u>, 77.7 on your A.M. radio dial. And visit our web site at www. chr. comm. so you can learn all about WCHR and review the conversations we've had over the years.

RADIO SHOW FOR JUNE 20th, 1997

Announcer: We have in our studio Pastor Jehoram from Jerusalem. How was you flight, Pastor J.?

Pastor Jehoram: It was a great flight. It was so fascinating I got an idea for a book called Flying Over Cities And Countries.

Announcer: Do you think you will ever write that book? And what would it be about?

Pastor Jehoram: It would be a fictional book about a pilot who flies different passengers all over the world.

Announcer: What would be so different about this book?

Pastor Jehoram: The pilot is an opera singer and he performs by singing selections of different operas.

Announcer: And the passengers don't mind?

Pastor Jehoram: Not at all. They join in on the chorouses they know, making everyone at ease and having a good time in the air.

Announcer: You are so creative! What kind of books do you read, for pleasure?

Pastor Jehoram: I read biographies, and auto-biographies, mainly. I like non-fiction, for the most part.

5
5

Announcer: Do you like writing?

Pastor Jehoram: Sometimes I think it's futile to write. No one cares about what I say or how I say it. All I am is a sermon machine. People are surprized when I tell them I write fiction. I wish people would stop assuming that sermons is all I write. I'm to the point where I could very easily write a bio of my own called Don't You Listen?
It would be about how I encourage the people to follow the Lord, and only a few people listen.

Announcer: Someone listens. That's what maffers.

Pastor Jehoram: I did assemble a book of photgraphs of fruit called Good Stuff! I took the pictures in black and white to show the contrasts in colors, such as the light color of a banana, as compared to the dark color of an apple. It took me years to learn how to get the lighting just right.

5
6

Announcer:     How long have you been taking photographs?

Pastor Jehoram: About ten years. When the fun of it became work I decided to slow down a lot.

Announcer: Good for you. I understand you like to read poems as part of your sermons.

Pastor Jehoram: Yes, I do read an occassional poem.

Announcer: Will you share one with the listening audience?

Pastor Jehoram: I'd love to. I recived one in the mail by a parishoner called <u>What Man Thinks He Has No Need For God?</u> This one was just the right one for my sermon called God Made Adam And Eve. I'll only read a stanza of the poem.

Announcer: That's fine. You read as the Spirit leads.

5
7

Pastor Jehoram: We need to have the formalities of Sunday services toned down to the point where love rules in every church. We need to put more prayer in our prayer services, by not necessarily going by a prayer list, but allowing the Spirit to pray through us. We need to be more Christ-like in our walk, and remember what He saved us from.

Announcer: And you are listening to WCHR, 77.7 on your A.M. radio dial. You can visit us at our website, on the Internet, at www. chr. comm. Also, don't forget to watch Public Access at 7am and 7pm for the show called Interviewin~ The Clerov.

RADIO SHOW FOR JUNE 21st, 1997

Announcer: Pastor Kish, from Kenya, welcome to our studios here at WCHR. How was the flight?

Pastor Kish: Long, tiring, and hot!

5
9

Announcer:  Tell the listening audience about the church you are the pastor of.

Pastor Kish: The church I preach at is called The Church Of Our Commitment To God. It is a small church, but we all love and care about each other. And the love and caring is what makes the church grow. One member of the congregation told me that he was asked by a co-worker if he could come to church with him. "I want what you have inside of you," and now he's the pianist in the church I preach at.

Announcer:  It amazes me what God can do if we allow Him to love and care through us.

Pastor Kish: I'm always amazed at how God can use people, in small ways, or in big ways.

Announcer:  What else can you tell me about the church where God called you to preach.

60

Pastor Kish: We are open to the honest expressions of sincere believers who love the Lord.

One parishoner sent me a poem called <u>I Have Pledged My Life To Jesus</u>.

May I read a few lines for your listening audience?

Announcer: I'd love to hear it.

Pastor Kish: I have pledged my life to Jesus, giving Him all my strength; I want to do all I can for Him; I praise Him for all His blessings; I thank Him for everything He gives me.

Announcer: What line of the poem strikes you the most?

Pastor Kish: The line, "I want to do all I can for Him." It seems the author, no matter what went on in his life, wants to serve God

in a very humble way, not caring what anyone thinks.

Announcer: And you're listening to <u>WCHR</u>, 77.7 on your radio dial.

RADIO SHOW FOR JUNE 22nd, 1997.

Announcer: Today we have in our studios Pastor Lemuel, here from London as part of his preaching ministry. Dr. Lemuel wrote a book called God In Every Thought in which he describes life as a breathing devotion, since the thoughts carry into words, and words into deeds.
I read the book and I love it! The book expounds how we need to keep God in all of our thoughts so that we know He is there in every decision of life.

Pastor Lemuel: Thank you, kind sir, for that warm introduction.
I have also written God In Every Heart and The Greatness Of God.

6
2

On my radio show, Pastor Lemuel Hears From God, I read a lot of poetry. I receive poetry from my listeners all the time. One poem I especially like is called I Have Made Mv Peace With God. I think the author expressed how restless he was until God, like a gentle man, came into his heart.
May I read the first stanza?

Announcer: Yes, I'd like to hear what the author had to say.

Pastor Lemuel: I have made my peace with God, I had sleepless nights without the Savior; I have asked Him in my heart, I believe He bore all of my sins. Have you made your peace with Him today?

Announcer: It is interesting how the author ends the stanza by asking if the reader has made his peace with God.

63

Pastor Lemuel: Yes, and I think the author has a heart for lost souls. Maybe that's why he asked that question of the reader.

It seems the author wants to give the reader spiritual food for thought.
I wrote a short one act play entitled Peace With God, about a person who was an atheist, and decided to repent of his unbelief. In the play the atheist argues with God, as a monologue, but God does nothing but listen.

Announcer: Have you done anything with your play?

Pastor Lemuel: I've had it performed numerous times over the past year. God has used it mainly for the back-sudden Christians who stopped caring about church, the Bible, and any Christian activity.

Announcer: You're listening to Pastor Lemuel from London as he talks about how God is mightily using him in his ministry. Pastor Lemuel: I have written another book that was on my heart for years.

Announcer: And it is entitled?

Pastor Lemuel: It is entitled When A Christian Loves Money More Than God. I use as a premise on how the constant hoarding of money by some well meaning professing Christians not only ruins their testimony, but it also ruins the chance of anyone who does not know Jesus, to come to Him.

Announcer: I think the Christian who loves money could care less about anything but money, and the over-accumulation of assets and the upsetting feeling of buying anything for anyone, ever.

65

Pastor Lemuel: You got the point of my book. I hope the listeners buy it as it is only $8.95, and onlytwo-hundred pages long.

Announcer: Thank you, Pastor Lemuel, for all of your insights concerning spiritual maffers.

RADIO SHOW FOR JUNE 23rd, 1997

Announcer: We have in our studios today Pastor Malachi from Maine. He is the pastor of The Church Of Burdens Lifted, in the small town of Lightload, Maine. Welcome to our studios, Pastor Malachi.

Pastor Malachi: It is such a pleasure to be here.

Announcer: How did the church you preach at get its name?

Pastor Malachi: I got a phone call one day and there was weeping on the other end of the line. A woman was distraught about how her life was going, so she decided to give up all hope. I asked if it was okay to come see her since she was so upset. She said fine. We ended up talking for hours about all her problems till she said, "You lifted all my burdens today." So, after much discussion, we decided to call the church The Church Of Burdens Lifted. There are so many hearts out there that need a listening ear. All we do in our church services is hear out every person that has a burden, and we pray till the burden is lighter, or even lifted.

Announcer:     Don't you even have an order of worship?

Pastor Malachi: No, our order of worship is the burdens that we help all our parishoners carry.

Announcer: Is there any healing from your listening?

Pastor Malachi: Oh, yes, very much so. We have prevented numerous people from calling it a life, since they were at the end of their ropes.

Announcer: What if some people resist your help?

Pastor Malachi: There is nothing I can do offer doing all I can. I just pray till they see the light.

Announcer: I understand that you wrote a book called Short Stories For Pastors When The Well Is Dry. Will you tell our listeners about it?

Pastor Malachi: I based this book on obscure book called <u>Poems For Pastors</u>.

6
8

I have borrowed about thirty poem titles to write short stories. I think people will like it.

Announcer: Will you share a short story?

Pastor Malachi: I would rather read the poem that inspired the short story. The poem is only one stanza, while the story goes on for pages.

Announcer:    Good, read the poem. I guess you'll be selling your book, too, like all the other guests on my show.

Pastor Malachi: Yes, I did write Stories For Pastors, and no I will be not be plugging it on your fine radio station. I thought you understood that I'm hear to bear burdens. Will you tell me yours?

Announcer:    I feel like I'm a soap box for every preacher who ever wrote a book. Instead of getting to the heart of the matter

6
9

all they ever do is plug their little self-published books.

Pastor Malachi: I realized your intent was to minister to everyone through inviting pastors on your radio show. Right?

Announcer: Yes, that is right.

Pastor Malachi: May I tell some people off?

Announcer: Be my guest.

Pastor Malachi: Pastors, please use other marketing tools for pushing your well written, well thought out music or books. Our friend here loves it when you talk about the church, and how you are ministering in the church. Please refrain from using valuable air time for plugging any item that you need to market elsewhere.

Announcer: Thank you. You're listening to WCHR, 77.7 on you A.M. radio dial.

Pastor Malachi: Can I read one stanza of the poem I mentioned earlier?

Announcer: I'd love to hear it, since it's only part of a poem.

Pastor Malachi: God bless!
Will you come to know the Lord? You only have to admit your need for Him. Why not shun your pride and Come to know Jesus as your Friend. All you have to do is repent of sin.

Announcer: That was an interesting work of poetry. What line did you like the most?

Pastor Malachi: I liked the line, "Why not shun your pride?" The author seems to get to the root of the spiritual problem by saying, 'Forget your pride and get it together with the Lord.'

7
1

Announcer: And you're listening to <u>WCHR</u>, 77.7 on your A.M. radio dial. RADIO SHOW FOR JUNE 24th. 1997

Announcer: We have in our studios Pastor Nahum from Nigeria. Pastor Nahum preaches at the Our Lord Is Abundantly Merciful Church.
What is the basic focus of your ministry at the church where you were called to preach?

Pastor Nahum: Our basic outreach is compassion.
We care deeply for every person we meet, since every person is our neighbor.

Announcer: How do you reach out to the people in your neighborhood?

Pastor Nahum: We go to homes for the blind to read to them, whatever book they want to listen to. Just seeing their

expressions is worth it for us. We also teach people how to read so they could read whatever they want, whenever they want. Along with teaching people how to read, we teach them how to write so that they can function in a world that has embraced the computer.

Announcer: It seems you have a full ministry.

Pastor Nahum: Yes, and we also make it a point to give food and clothes to any person who may need them.

Announcer: What do you preach on?

Pastor Nahum: I usually have a prepared text and homily that I deliver on subjects ranging from abstinenance to victory. If the Spirit moves me to not use my notes, then I preach what is in my heart.

Announcer: That's nice, but what do you preach on?

73

Pastor Nahum: When I preach on sin, which is unheard of in the late nineties, I get laughed at.
When I say repent, it doesn't mean a thing. I have to have a multi-media presentation to maybe gain some people's interest, and wake them from their sleep.

Announcer: How sad. Why is the church so lethargic?

Pastor Nahum: All anyone cares for is ritual. Be it the ritual of a rigid church service or the ritual of any element that is brought into a sacred service to bring one closer to God.

Announcer: I understand you write poetry. Do you have a poem or two with you?

Pastor Nahum: I do have one poem that a parishoner wrote and put in the offering plate with a note saying, "This is my gift from God to you. God bless." It is called, I <u>Shall Always Wait For Him</u>.

I shall always wait for Him to come for me, and take me Home; He will someday come for all On a day that only God knows.

Announcer: What line from this poem meant a lot to you?

Pastor Nahum: I liked the line 'He will someday come.' Waiting for the rapture seems very hard to do in the nineties since it doesn't seem to be a subject from most pulpits. If we forget about Jesus as our hope, then what's left?

Announcer: You have said some thought-provoking things. It seems there aren't very many serious thinkers any more. Some people hear a few statements and label it as fact before checking it out. And you're listening to WCHR, 77.7 on your A.M. radio dial.

Pastor Nahum: I think every Christian should show real mercy and compassion towards all other people, and should stop judging

every one based on their little isolated text of Scripture. At our church our love is unconditional and our mercy towards our fellow men is the pursuit of following the Lord's example of mercy as much as we can.

Announcer: I think standing up for Jesus is better than following any church rules.

Pastor Nahum: It seems that some verses of the Bible is ignored while others are grasped and taken too closely to heart, like a live-what-you-like philosophy which is not very healthy.

Announcer: We are all out of time, Pastor Nahum. We will have you back sometime in the future, Lord willing.

RADIO SHOW FOR JUNE 25th, 1997

Announcer: We have in our studios today Pastor Onam, from Oregon. Welcome to our studios Pastor Onam. I understand you

were called to preach at The Church With The Loving Heart.
Will you tell the radio audience about the church?

Pastor Onam: At The Church With The Loving Heart we love every individual, with an unconditional love. We encourage gentle hugs and firm handshakes. We encourage people to edify each other, by conversation that is pleasing to the Lord.

Announcer: And what if someone chooses not to?

Pastor Onam: If someone chooses not to be an encouragement to a fellow brother, then all we can do is pray for him.

Announcer: Is there any set of rules for encouraging a brother?

Pastor Onam: There's no set of rules or basic guidelines, but loving is a priority.

Announcer: What about personality clashes between parishoner and parishoner, parishoner and song leader, song leader and pastor, and so on.

Pastor Onam: Each situation is handled carefully and prayerfully so as not to hurt any person s ego. One time we talked for hours as to how to present a musical called <u>We Live To Love Our Lord</u>.

Announcer: Was it worth the hours of conversation?

Pastor Onam: Yes, we have had to compromise on some songs so as to reach the youth and the elderly, but the end result was beautiful!

Announcer: I realize you cannot please everyone. No matter how loving a church is someone will still find fault.

Pastor Onan: We basically worry about loving the Lord first of all, and, we do our

7
8

best to love our brothers, whether or not we are loved in return; whether or not we are understood.

Announcer: Could you tell our radio audience the lyrics to <u>We Live To Love Our Lord</u>?

Pastor Onam: We live to love our Lord, with voice in one accord; We live to serve the One who put His love in our hearts, praying He gives us grace to love every one we meet, to love every one we meet.

Announcer: I understand that the musical has aired on the Public Access and The Religion Channel for the past six months. Why do you think it is so popular?

Pastor Onam: It talks about people living to love the Lord no matter what their lot in life is.

Announcer: And who wrote the musical?

7
9

Pastor Onam: A 43 year old Italian man who loves the Lord very much, and would like to see other people find real reasons to love Him.

Announcer: You don't know his name?

Pastor Onam: It doesn't matter. What matters is the message, not the messenger.

Announcer: And you're listening to <u>WCHR</u>, 77.7 on your A.M. radio dial. Please watch my television show Interviewing The Clergy. It airs at 7AM and 7PM daily. Check your program guide for listings in your area.

RADIO SHOW FOR JUNE 26th, 1997.

Announcer: We have in our studios today Pastor Philetus from Pennsylvania. Welcome to our studios. Tell us about the church where you accepted the call to preach.

Pastor Philetus: The name of the church where I preach is called The Lord Is First In All Things.

We do our best to serve the Lord in The Lord Is First In All Things Fellowship.

We are not a perfect church. I am not a perfect pastor.

It is our goal to see the family work in harmony, without devoting every waking hour to the church. We need to have every part of our lives in perspective, never emphasizing one part over another. If the family works in harmony with God, then church and work will all be in harmony.

Announcer: Some people do put church and church service above their families? Why is that?

Pastor Philetus: Probably because they want affention, or maybe their love for God is so deep the person would ignore the home for the church.

Announcer: Where is the balance for people?
How can it be affained?

Pastor Philetus: The individual has to question his own actions as to how he lives his life. Some people over-do every thing, other people over-do by doing nothing. There is no middle ground with some people.

Announcer: What do you like about pastoring a church?

Pastor Philetus: I like the interaction with my congregation on a weekly basis. When I lead Bible studies, prayer meetings, or visit the sick I also have that time with them.

Announcer: Since you are a pastor, do you think you are any closer to God than the average Christian?

Pastor Philetus: I never gave that much thought. I do know that it is an enormous responsibility to preach The Word of God, God's Word, to people, and that I am

responsible for the way I expound His Word, and that I have to give an account of my life to Him, for every word said.

Announcer: You must care deeply for the flock you were called to shepherd.

Pastor Philetus: I care so much I am graciously called 'beloved' by a few in the church.

Announcer: People know whether or not they are loved. You seem to care very much for people.

Pastor Philetus: You know, I almost became a doctor because I cared enough to help the sick get well. I became a minister because I wanted to help in the healing of lost souls.
May I read part of a poem that a young man sent to the church? It is called <u>You Must Seek Him Now</u>.

Announcer: I'm sure we'd all love to hear the poem. Yes, you may read it.

Pastor Philetus: You must seek Him now. The way the world is, rejecting the Truth, The rapture could take place tomorrow. You could be here, alone, Why are you living without the Lord in your life? Now is the time.

Announcer: Do you read a lot of poems people send you?

Pastor Philetus: I read about three a year. I do not let any author's poetry stand in the way of The Bible. As a maffer of fact, I always ask God to bless the reading of His Word. I ask Him in different ways every Sunday, so as to be sure He gets all the glory. I am a messenger of the message. I use every resouece available to build up my brothers in the Lord, and to lead sinners to repentance.

Announcer: You are tuned to <u>WCHR</u>, 77.7 on your A.M. radio dial. Visit our web site at www.wchr.comm. Each show is transcribed so you can print out the ones that mean the most to you.

RADIO SHOW FOR JUNE 27th, 1997.

Announcer: We have in our studios Pastor Quartus from Quebec, Canada. Thank you for coming from Quebec to Miami Beach. Tell us all about your ministry.

Pastor Quartus: I was called to preach at The Caring And Kindness Life Church. We make it a point to care about every person and show kindness no matter how they are dressed or how they walk or talk. Our kindness is unconditional.

Announcer: Unconditional kindness is rare in the late nineties. It seems people have to

meet certain criteria to be part of certain churches. Don't you have an amazing diversity by opening your doors to every person?

Pastor Quartus: We are just following our Lord's example in that caring and kindness is how He lived his life.

Announcer: What about the day He cleared the temple? What about the time He called the scribes and pharisees names?

Pastor Quartus: Caring and kind acts do not always mean kind deeds or words. In one instance He looked out for His Father. In the other instance He called it like it was, showing people what they could not see in themselves.

Announcer: Is there an instance when you needed to set aside your caring or kindness?

Pastor Quartus: No, but one instance I do remember was this man who was told to see a doctor time and time again by a fellow parishoner. The man got belier as time passed, but the parishoner died. It was her time to go. She was outwardly insistant, bordering on being cruel, since she cared so much, knowing the man could die. She saved his life. Now he's happier, and healthier.

Announcer: I guess caring and kindness have many sides. We need to ask the Lord for wisdom in expressing that daily to our fellow man.

Pastor Quartus: I brought a poem that I'd like to share. It is entitled, <u>When Will You Listen To The Lord</u>? Before I read this I want the radio listeners to understand that you must base what people say on the Bible, as a solid frame of reference. If what a person says is of the Lord, and it isn't, then the person is not very reliable.

It is good to be skeptical and critical when
anyone says, 'the Lord says' unless it is in

The Holy Bible. One example is a so-called spiritual Christian man insisted that Miss Smith and Mr. Jones marry. They did, and they divorced within six months.

Listening to the Lord should be in the context of The Holy Bible, prayer, and sometimes fasting. No one should jump to any conclusions concerning the life of any one. More people need to hear from God for guidance. I pray people listen and hear Him. The poem: When will you listen to the Lord, by reading the Bible, His Word; Will you do His perfect will? You do not have forever to heed His call. You only have today.

Announcer: Why did you emphasize on whether or not a person hears from God?

Pastor Quartus: Because there are thousands of other voices that are very tempting. People need to concentrate on shuffing out the other voices and listen to the Bible being read on a daily basis.

Announcer: What about the people who have read the Bible ten or more times and have listened to it five times? And what if they remain unchanged by His Word?

Pastor Quartus: If a man has only a head knowledge of The Word Of God, and he can quote it forwards and backwards, and he doesn't apply it, then how can The Bible be hidden in his heart? I guess it is better to memorize a few verses and hide them in your heart, then to read the whole Bible ten times and apply nothing.

Announcer: You are listening to WCHR, 77.7 on your A.M. radio dial.

RADIO SHOW FOR JUNE 28TH, 1997.

Announcer: We have in our studios today
Pastor Rephael from Richmond, Virginia.

8
9

tempting. People need to concentrate on shuffing out the other voices and listen to the Bible being read on a daily basis.

Announcer: What about the people who have read the Bible ten or more times and have listened to it five times? And what if they remain unchanged by His Word?

Pastor Quartus: If a man has only a head knowledge of The Word Of God, and he can quote it forwards and backwards, and he doesn't apply it, then how can The Bible be hidden in his heart? I guess it is better to memorize a few verses and hide them in your heart, then to read the whole Bible ten times and apply nothing.

Announcer: You are listening to <u>WCHR</u>, 77.7 on your A.M. radio dial.

RADIO SHOW FOR JUNE 28TH, 1997.

Announcer: We have in our studios today Pastor Rephael from Richmond, Virginia.

Welcome to our studios Pastor. Tell us about the church where you are minister.

Pastor Rephael: The name of the church is The God Will Heal You Someday Fellowship.

Announcer: How did the church get its name?

Pastor Rephael: We are evangelical in our nature. We visit the sick daily and give them hope that they will be healed of whatever. We do not ever promise any one a healing. All we do is give hope.

Announcer: How do you give a dying person hope?

Pastor Rephael: We read every instance where God ever healed a person from the book of Genesis to the book of Revelation.

Announcer: How long does that take?

9
0

Pastor Rephael: As long as the sick or dying person wants. We tell the person the healing passages of Scripture, and, if the person can, he or she chooses them. We then read what is chosen.

Announcer: This could go on for hours, right?

Pastor Rephael: No, not really. We can sense when it is time to stop.

Announcer: How many sick or dying were healed since you began ministering in this way?

Pastor Rephael: At least one hundred. The hospitals anticipate empty beds a day or two after we leave.

Announcer: Does the patient anticipate geffing better?

Pastor Rephael: Yes, since the television or radio is on the patient still has vivid scenes of examples where God did the healing.

Announcer: And there is no doubt in your mind that God does heal?

Pastor Rephael: There is no doubt in my mind. The doctors check out each patient completely before releasing any one. Ours is not a healing service where we act as vessels for God's power to flow through us, all we do is read, what I like to call, is The Healing Examples.

Announcer: And when there is no healing at all?

Pastor Rephael: Then we know that we have offered hope. A liffle bit of hope is belier than no hope at all.

Announcer: You are tuned to <u>WCHR</u>, 77.7 on your A.M. radio dial.

RADIO SHOW FOR JUNE 29th, 1997.

9
2

Announcer: We have in our studios today Pastor Serah, who came here from San Diego, California.
Tell us about the church where you minister.

Pastor Serah: As a lady minister I am always asking the Lord for strength and wisdom in how to encourage people on His day. The name on the church is The Church Of Honoring Our Lord. It is only as we honor Him that we are blessed in abundance.

Announcer: How did God lead you to The Church Of Honoring Our Lord?

Pastor Serah: The search committee chose me over four other applicants. I guess they saw something in me that could help their walk with the Lord.

Announcer: Isn't that what the church is all about? Not fancy pews or a fancy choir. Not elegant carpeting or hand carved crosses. Not paintings of Our Lord or many saints. The church is about our walk with the Lord.

Pastor Serah: It seems to me some churches are very simple in architecture and props, if you will. Other churches go all out to honor Him. You are right, though, if the props that you refer to hinder one man's walk with the Lord, then it seems the man needs to focus more on Him than the props of the house of worship, no matter how meaningful.

Announcer: You seem to have a remarkable sense of observation about things.

Pastor Serah: I guess it is all what you choose to care about. If you care more for the stained glass than the One who gave people the wisdom to make stained glass, then things are not in perspective.

Announcer: It is not easy to put the church, as a unit, in proper perspective. It seems pastors stay a short time, then leave. Parishoners stay a short time, then leave.

Churches change names since things fall apart sometimes. Why is that?

Pastor Serah: The Bible says when Jesus comes back He will find a glorious church, without spot or wrinkle. I think the Lord is just ironing out a few wrinkles, and washing out every spot, so that it will be glorious.

Announcer: What about the Christians who walked away from God, for whatever reason.

Pastor Serah: It is their choice to walk with Him or not. If a Christian is no longer walking with God, he needs to rethink why he became a Christian in the first place, and rethink why not walking with God seems to be better. I pray for those who trust the messenger more than the One the message is about. It grieves me that we, the messenger, are held in high esteem, so much so that Jesus is obscured.

Announcer: How do you honor the Lord?

Pastor Serah: I have different members of our congregation say how they honored God, only the people that want to. We have no fixed order of worship. When I read a Scripture I ask for a person in the church who knows more than I, to talk about it. You see, the church is full of talented people. We honor God by encouraging the person with one talent or five talents to use them with all his might. Sunday nights is when short stories are told, or poems are read, or even art work displayed, or liftle rock 'n roll operas are performed. We do not stifle any one. We water each others talents so that the church will also grow, and that the world will be blessed.

Announcer: What if someone has an off the wall idea?

Pastor Serah: We dilligently and gently work with each individual before any item is even by the sacred pulpit. We need to screen. We just cannot let anyone ramble on and on without being talked to first.

Announcer: Is this a form of censorship?

Pastor Serah: No, we need to honor God as a church. What a man writes is his own opinion, but people see and hear every thing from a different point of view. What is said from the pulpit has numerous implications, but what is said in a book only affects the reader. It is an enormous responsibility to pastor a church.

Announcer: We are all out of time. We had in our studios Pastor Serah, from San Diego, California, talking to us about the church where she ministers. This is <u>WCHR</u>, 77.7 on your A.M. radio dial.

RADIO SHOW FOR JUNE 30th, 1997.

Announcer: We have in our studios Pastor Tiras from Tennessee. Pastor, tell us about your church and ministry.

Pastor Tiras: The name of the church where I minister is The Hope Of Our Lord's Appearing. We make it a point to talk about the rapture of the saints on a weekly basis, always making sure people understand that how a person lives is very important. Some moral people come to our church and it has not dawned on them yet that they need Jesus as their Savior before they can be raptured.

Announcer: Do you relate other Bible passages to the rapture?

Pastor Tiras: As Much as I can. For example, I preached on Noah and the ark, and said, 'Once we are raptured and with the Lord, we can ask Noah what it was like to hear His voice and build such a great vessel.'

Announcer: Through regular Bible stories you still emphasize the importance of the rapture. Why?

Pastor Tiras: I do not want it to be a forgotten doctrine. As a preacher I need to preach the whole Word of God, and not spend a year on John Chapter One.

Announcer: It seems like making people think for themselves is a part of your ml nistry.

Pastor Tiras: I offer things to ponder from the pulpit. I never tell any one what to think or how to think. It is my responsibility to love people into Heaven without screaming or yelling. If no hope is offered, then people leave church empty.

Announcer: No matter what name is on the door some person still has title to the land and access to the building. The money is counted weekly and

distributed accordingly. Don't people ultimately run the church?

Pastor Tiras: The Lord graciously puts someone in charge to collect and distribute the money. He is the head of the church only as people are willing to follow Him.

Announcer: And if no one listens to Him?

Pastor Tiras: If the church merrily walks without Him then eventually it will crumble. I have seen a few churches crumble, and it is not pretty. I tire of the useless bickering over the color of a hymnal or how songs are presented or what songs are presented. And, in the meantime, lost souls drop into hell, since the church acts just like the world.

Announcer: And you are tuned to WCHR, 77.7 on your A.M. radio dial.